Dunc's Undercover Christmas

Gary Paulsen

Dunc's Undercover Christmas

A YEARLING BOOK

Published by
Dell Publishing
a division of
Bantam Doubleday Dell Publishing Group, Inc.
1540 Broadway
New York, New York 10036

ISBN: 0-440-40874-1

Printed in the United States of America

October 1993

10 9 8 7 6 5 4 3 2 1

OPM

Dunc's Undercover Christmas

Chapter · 1

Duncan—Dunc—Culpepper and Amos Binder, his best friend for life, were sitting on the old couch in Dunc's basement. Dunc was replacing the burned-out bulbs in last year's Christmas tree lights. He carefully unwound each strand. Plugged it in. Checked, cleaned, and tightened each bulb.

Amos was sure that Dunc was spending too much time on this job. After all, what was a burned-out bulb here and there? But he knew Dunc. Dunc was neat and precise to the point of driving Amos crazy. He also knew it would be next to impossible to rush him—even on a beautiful day in the middle of December, when they should be outside having fun.

Amos waited. He scratched his neck. He rubbed up and down against the back of the couch. Then he really let go. He slid down to the floor and rolled around like a puppy.

Dunc watched him a few minutes. "That's a bad rash. How did you get it?"

"From the grocery store."

"You got a rash from the grocery store?"

"Well—sort of." Amos sat up. "I was following my mom down the cereal aisle. If I don't go to the store with her, she comes home with all kinds of junk. You know, vegetables and green stuff."

Dunc nodded.

"Anyway—I was in the cereal aisle picking up a couple of boxes of Fruit Slams, when it happened."

"What?"

"The phone rang. I could tell it was Melissa. She has that different sort of—sharp, bell-like, ring. I always know when it's her."

Dunc nodded again. Melissa Hansen was Amos's dream girl. As far as Amos was concerned, she was the most perfect girl in the world. He was always certain she was calling him. Dunc knew that Melissa had not called Amos at the grocery store. Not just because Amos was in the grocery store but mainly because Melissa Hansen didn't even know Amos's name. And from all indications didn't want to.

"Well, since it was Melissa calling for me, I thought I'd save everybody some time and get it myself. I let go of the Fruit Slams. Took a shortcut over Mrs. Bundy's grocery cart—she got a little excited when I stepped on her bread—and from there on it was pure instinct."

Dunc was positive that somewhere in Amos's genetic makeup was a wild gene that caused him to go stone crazy whenever he heard a telephone ring. He couldn't prove it, but someday he intended to do a study on it. It would be a long study, with notes and reams of information, and each point would be catalogued and subcatalogued, and—

"I climbed out of Mrs. Bundy's cart right up on the top shelf of canned goods. It was great. I could see the whole store from up there. I wish you could have seen me. I was in perfect form. Right foot down, arms up, head back. Class act all the way. I had a fix on the phone and was closing in. Then things started to go wrong."

Dunc took out another bulb. "What happened?"

"Spinach. Cans of spinach. They started rolling underneath me. I couldn't stop. I took a nosedive and wiped out the whole top shelf."

Dunc frowned. "I don't get it. What caused the rash?"

"When the shelf ended, I kept going. Right over the fruit and vegetable section. I landed headfirst in the middle of the strawberries. That's what did it. I'm allergic."

"Did you ever get to the phone?"

"No. By the time I crawled out of those slimy strawberries, Melissa had already hung up. She's particular that way. She likes me to pick it up on that all-important first ring."

Dunc shook his head. "That's too bad. About Melissa, I mean. What did the store manager say?"

"That's the funny part. I figured he'd be upset. At least want me to pay for some of the damage. But he didn't. He just stood there and made a noise sort of like the one Scruff makes when he has to go out. Oh, he asked my mom if she would consider shopping over at that new supermarket across town. Don't you think that's kind of weird? Asking a steady customer to shop somewhere else?"

Dunc put in the last bulb. "Well, I guess that does it. What do you want to do now?"

Amos stopped scratching. "I still have some Christmas shopping to do." He looked at his watch. "And it's about time for Melissa to get out of dance class. If we start for the mall now, we'll probably pass her coming out of Miss Borgia's studio."

Dunc ignored the part about Melissa. "I thought you had all your Christmas shopping finished."

"I do. At least, I have my family finished. I bought my mom this really cool basketball. I got my dad a new video cartridge. And I bought Amy the best thing of all: a game of Laser Chase."

"I can see that you really put a lot of thought into choosing your gifts," Dunc said.

"Yeah. It's tough. You wouldn't want to spend all that money and see stuff just lie around not being used. I try extra hard to get things a person really wants."

"And if that person just happens to be you . . ."

Amos grinned. "Isn't Christmas great?"

Dunc shook his head. "I worry about you." He stacked the strands of Christmas lights neatly on a shelf. "Who else do you need to shop for?"

"My cousin T.J. He's coming to visit for the holidays."

"I've heard you talk about him. He's a little younger than us, isn't he?"

"Yeah, a year or so. But he's a neat guy. His dad is African American. His great-grandmother still lives in Ethiopia. She taught him to speak Amharic. That's her native language. He's always quoting old Amharic proverbs. But they lose a little something in the English translation."

"What does 'T.J.' stand for?"

"His whole name is Theodore James Tyler. But the only one who can call him that and get away with it is his great-grandmother."

"When's he going to get here?" Dunc asked.

"He should be here day after tomorrow. I think you're really going to like him. He invents things."

"What kind of things?"

"Oh, all kinds of things. You'll see when you meet him. His dad's some kind of scientist. I guess T.J. takes after him."

Amos looked at his watch again. "Come on. I'll tell you more about him on the way to the mall. If we don't hurry, I'll miss my chance to wave at her."

Dunc thought about telling him how pointless it was. That Melissa wouldn't recognize him, and even if she did, she wouldn't wave at him. He started to.

Instead he shook his head and followed Amos out the door.

Chapter · 2

The mall was ablaze with bright reds and greens. A Santa was taking Christmas Eve orders from small, wide-eyed children. The stores were bursting at the seams with shoppers. Christmas was definitely here.

"Too bad Melissa didn't notice you," Dunc said.

Amos was looking at a remote-control robot. "Yeah. Next time I'll have to try a little harder to get her attention."

Dunc smiled. "You would have thought stopping traffic and waving that fluorescent yellow 'Hello Melissa' banner would do the trick."

"She was busy with her friends."

"So I noticed."

Amos ignored him and kept playing with the robot.

"Are you thinking about getting that for T.J.?" Dunc asked.

"This? Heck no. He could probably build ten of these himself."

"Then why are you wasting our time looking at it?"

"It's not a waste of time." Amos made the robot go in little circles. "I check out stuff. You know, in case someone hasn't bought my gift yet and they need some suggestions. Speaking of gifts, have you bought me one yet?"

"What makes you think I'm going to get you a gift?"

"Come off it! You always get me something." Amos looked worried. "You *are* getting me a gift, aren't you?"

Dunc's eyes had a mischievous look. "Yes and no."

"What does that mean?"

"It means I'm getting you something. But I don't have all the details worked out yet."

"What kind of a present has details to work out?"

Dunc changed the subject. "Have you thought of anything for T.J. yet?"

"Oh, that's easy. A gift certificate from the electronics store. He spends most of his time building different gadgets. I'm sure he can use some spare parts."

"The electronics store is at the other end of the mall." Dunc pulled on his sleeve.

"Okay, okay. Give me a minute. Let me take one last test run around this aisle."

Dunc sighed. "Try to hurry."

Amos and the robot rounded the corner. They were making their way through the pet section when Amos accidentally pushed the fast-forward button. The robot took off. It ran smack into someone's black boot.

Amos looked up. It was Santa. Or rather

a man dressed in a Santa suit with a long white beard.

He winked at Amos. "This what you want for Christmas, son? Well, I'm the man to talk to about it. Of course, you haven't been all that good this year, have you?"

Amos stared at the Santa. His mouth was hanging wide open.

"Let's see. There was that unfortunate problem with your dog." The Santa laughed. "And there's the incident involving your sister's diary. But who knows?" He winked. "I may stop by your house anyway."

The Santa reached down, picked up the robot, and handed it to Amos. "Take care you don't test run the battery down." Then he walked down the aisle ringing a silver bell and saying, "Ho, ho, ho."

Amos watched him until he was out of sight. Then he blasted around the corner to the counter where Dunc was waiting.

"What took you—" Dunc started.

Amos interrupted, "You won't believe it —Santa—real—he knows!"

Dunc frowned at him. "Calm down. What happened?"

Amos started again. "He's real. He knows things about me. I thought he was only for little kids or dweebs, but he's really *real*."

Dunc scratched his head. "Are you okay? Maybe we'd better get you home. Let you get some rest. We can shop later."

"No. You don't understand. Santa—I met the real Santa. He told me things."

"Is that all? Those guys are paid to tell you things. They tell everybody the same things over and over."

Amos grabbed the front of Dunc's coat. "Listen to me. This one knew real-life things about me."

"Amos."

"He knew about my dog and my sister."

"Get real, Amos. Those are common things. He made a good guess. Don't let it spook you."

"I don't know. . . ."

"Come on. I'll buy you a soda. You need

it. What would Melissa say if she heard you carrying on about a real Santa Claus?"

Amos's shoulders slumped. "Maybe you're right. I lost it there for a minute. He caught me off guard with some of that stuff. Don't worry, I'm okay now. Uh—Dunc?"

"Yeah?"

"Let's keep this just between us. Okay?"

"No problem."

Chapter·3

Amos chucked a basketball at the hoop above his garage door. It bounced off the rim. He caught it on the way down. Dribbled to the end of the driveway, and turned to face the basket.

A dreamy look came to his face. He was in the game of his life, standing at the free-throw line. A hush came over the crowd. The score was tied with only two seconds left on the clock. It was the last chance for his team to score. The winning point rested

on his shoulders. He bounced the ball. Once.
Twice. Took careful aim. And he—

"Amos."

—missed.

Dunc rode up in the driveway waving a
newspaper.

"Aw, man!" Amos stomped his foot. "You
just ruined our only chance to win the
game."

Dunc looked around. He sat back on his
bike. "The game?"

"Never mind." Amos picked up the ball.
"What were you yelling about?"

"Take a look at this." Dunc unfolded the
paper and pointed to an article.

Amos read the headline out loud: " 'Store
Robbed by Shoplifting Santa.' " He handed
the paper back. "Want to play a little one-
on-one?"

"Don't you get it?" Dunc asked.

"No, I don't get it. And I don't *want* to get
it. Let me tell you why. Because every time
you read something in the newspaper, you
get us involved. And that always means

trouble. Like the time you read about that chemical stuff at the dump. And I was attacked by dead bodies and had to run around town dressed up like garbage."

"You were not attacked, you just thought you were. And we were dressed in camouflage."

Amos bounced the ball.

"We were in this store yesterday," Dunc said.

Amos shrugged. "So?"

"You saw a Santa."

"I saw about a dozen Santas yesterday."

Dunc pointed to the paper. "The article puts the robbery at about the same time we were in the department store. You may have actually seen the Santa who ripped them off."

"No."

"What do you mean—no?"

"I mean no. It couldn't have been him. He wouldn't do something like that."

"Amos. You're not back on that *real* Santa kick again, are you?"

"All I'm saying is that I talked to him—you didn't. There was something about him. He didn't seem the type."

Dunc folded up the newspaper. "Well, it's a lead, and I think we ought to check it out. The police aren't having much luck. Whoever this guy is, he shouldn't be allowed to get away with it. Especially at Christmas."

"Even if you're right—which I doubt—what could we do about it anyway?"

"I knew you'd be interested."

Amos held up his hand. "I never said I was interested. All I said was—"

Dunc interrupted, "I've decided to call it the Case of the Sticky-Fingered Santa."

Amos shook his head. "Here we go again. You're bound and determined to get us in some kind of mess, aren't you? It's what you live for." He handed Dunc the ball. "Let's shoot some free throws before we get too carried away with this detective stuff."

Dunc weighed the ball in his hand. Eyed the basket and carelessly tossed it through the hoop.

"How did you do that? I've never seen

18

you do that before!" Amos's eyes narrowed. "You've been holding out on me."

Dunc shrugged. "I've been studying angles of trajectory. I guess you could call that basket applied science. You see . . ."

The rest of his answer was drowned out when a blue and white van pulled up to the curb.

A man got out and started pulling suitcases out of the back. The side door opened. A short kid wearing a tan trench coat that hung almost to the ground stepped out.

"T.J.!" Amos yelled.

The kid grinned. "Hiya, Amos. Long time no see."

"T.J., I want you to meet my best friend in the whole world—Dunc Culpepper."

Dunc stuck out his hand. Amos saw the move and tried to warn him. It was too late. A flashing red light inched out of T.J.'s top coat pocket. Alarms started going off.

Dunc jumped back.

T.J. pressed a button. A voice said, "The time is ten o'clock."

T.J. looked up. "Wrong button." He

19

pressed another one. A boxing glove on the end of a spring popped out of his coat. He tried to stuff it back inside his coat, but it didn't want to go.

The neighbors were starting to come outside. Amos's dog, Scruff, trotted over and started barking. That set off a chain reaction. Dogs were barking up and down the street. T.J. kept pushing the wrong buttons. He couldn't get the alarm to shut off.

Dunc smiled. "I'd say you're Amos's cousin, all right. No doubt about that."

Chapter · 4

"I ran a check on all of the possible suspects." Dunc held up a list.

Amos shook his head. "Quit talking like you're with the FBI. All you did was call some department stores and ask where they get their Santas."

Dunc shrugged. "Same thing."

The three boys were in Dunc's room mapping out strategy for the case. Actually Dunc was talking strategy. T.J. was listening. And Amos was throwing darts and eating cheese puffs.

"Here's the deal," Dunc said. "Not all of the Santas who came in and out of the store on the robbery date can be accounted for. Some of them could have been doing charitable work. A few of them might have been shopping or working at some other store in the mall. Most of the stores I called hire their Santas from the Lundini Agency downtown. That's where we'll start. From there, it's a process of elimination. Simple."

"When he uses that word, watch out." Amos threw a dart at the board on Dunc's bedroom wall.

"This is so awesome." T.J. sat on the edge of the bed taking it all in. "My very first case. You guys are lucky, getting to do this all the time."

Amos snorted. "Lucky is not quite the word for it."

Dunc ignored him. "I've made arrangements for us to get inside the agency. Tomorrow we're supposed to report to a man

22

named Tyson. He's the manager. We'll get further directions from him."

"The manager is going to help us catch his own employees?" T.J. asked.

"Not exactly."

"See, I told you to watch out," Amos said.

Dunc shot Amos a look. "We're going to have to go undercover on this one."

"Wow!" T.J. jumped up. "You mean, like secret agents? This is getting better all the time. I've always wanted to go undercover. Do we get code names?"

Amos looked at him.

Dunc went on, "I let the agency manager think we're just kids who need some extra Christmas money. He said he could use us tomorrow for a special job."

Amos eyed him suspiciously. "Doing what?"

T.J. interrupted, "What does it matter, as long as we're in? What should I bring, Dunc? I have almost my entire supply with me."

"Entire supply?" Dunc asked.

"T.J. here comes fully equipped for any situation." Amos patted him on the back. "Automatic flyswatter, disappearing ink, remote-control lawn mower. You name it. He's invented it."

T.J. blushed. "Well, I don't know about every situation . . ."

"If you had a camera, one you could hide easily," Dunc said, "then we could get some pictures for the police."

"No problem." T.J. held out his hand. He flipped back the top of a large gold-colored ring on his middle finger. Inside was the smallest camera Dunc had ever seen.

Dunc moved over to inspect it. "Does it work?"

T.J. looked insulted. "Of course it works! Stand back, and I'll take your picture."

He closed the lid and pressed a hidden button on the top.

Dunc heard a tiny click. "Hey, that's all right, T.J. Just what we need."

He spoke too soon.

The lid on the ring snapped open. A small silver spring popped out. Then another. The film started unwinding. It curled up over the edge of the ring and fell out onto the floor.

T.J. shrugged. "I guess it still has a few bugs. But don't worry, I'll have them worked out by tomorrow. Like my great-grandmother always says, 'If it's worth doing, don't stand in the cow pasture.' Check you later." He started for the door.

Dunc leaned over to Amos. "What does that mean, exactly?"

Amos smiled and shrugged. "I don't know. I told you, it loses something in the translation. Don't worry, after you've been around him awhile, it starts to make sense."

Chapter · 5

"Elves? You told him we'd be elves? Are you crazy?"

Dunc shrugged. "It's a great disguise, Amos. This way, we can stay with the agency Santas all day, and no one will be suspicious. Besides, it was the only job available."

Amos looked at himself in the dressing-room mirror. He was green from head to toe. Green pointed hat. Green shirt. Green tights. Green slippers. "I am not going out

27

in public dressed like this, Dunc! I look like Peter Pan."

"No one will recognize you. It's Christmas, you'll blend in. Trust me."

"Ta-da!" T.J. jumped out of his dressing room. "How do I look, fellow detectives?"

Dunc frowned and shook his head. "You can't wear your trench coat, T.J. It doesn't go with the costume."

T.J.'s face fell. "But Dunc, I always wear it. I have to wear it. My entire life's work is in this coat. I can't *not* wear it."

"It's true," Amos said. "He always wears it. Even in the middle of summer."

Dunc looked at Amos. He looked at T.J. "Oh, all right. I guess it won't hurt anything. Come on. We'd better get going, or we'll be fired before we get started."

"Yes!" T.J. made a fist and pulled his elbow to his side. "You won't be sorry, Dunc. I may have some things in here that will help with the case."

"Don't." Dunc stopped and held up one finger. "Don't use any of your inventions unless it is an absolute emergency. Okay?"

"I'll be waiting for your signal. All you have to do is say the word."

"Right. Now, let's go. We're supposed to be at the Toy Emporium in ten minutes."

The store was only six blocks from the agency. The boys set out on their bikes. T.J. was riding Amy's bike. Which amazed Amos because she never let him—her own brother —near her bike. Or anything of hers, for that matter.

They walked their bikes across the street in front of a station wagon that was stopped at a red light.

Amos stared at the car. Melissa Hansen was sitting in the front seat. Melissa's mother was taking Melissa and some of her friends shopping. He started to wave. Then he remembered his costume. He froze in the middle of the street.

The light changed. Dunc yelled at him to come on. Amos couldn't move.

"Oh, brother." Dunc handed T.J. his bike. He went out into the street and led Amos to the curb. He sat him down on a bench and waited.

In a few seconds Amos came back to life. "Blend in. You said I'd blend in. She saw me —looking like a big green elf. I may kill you. A slow, painful death."

"Hold on. Chances are she didn't even recognize you. And if she did, well—she probably admires your Christmas spirit."

Amos stood up. He thought about it. "Do you really think so? I bet if we hurried, we could beat them to the next stoplight. I could walk across and—"

"Sorry, Amos. We have work to do."

T.J. moved up by Dunc. "What was that all about?"

"It's a long story. I'll fill you in when we have more time—there's the store."

They chained their bikes to a rack out front. Dunc and T.J. hurried inside to find the owner. Amos was right behind them until he felt a tap on his shoulder.

He turned around. It was Santa—the Santa from the mall.

"They really don't dress like that, you know," he said.

Amos looked around. "Who?"

"My elves."

"They don't?"

"No. They dress like everybody else. Confidentially, so do I. In the off season, of course."

"Amos!" Dunc was calling for him. "There you are. What are you doing out here?"

"Sorry, Dunc. I was talking to Santa."

"Santa?"

Amos turned to show him. The Santa was gone. "He was here a minute ago."

"You've been under a lot of stress lately, Amos. Maybe you should go on home. T.J. and I can handle the case."

"He was here, Dunc. Really. He told me how his elves really dress. It's not like this. You wouldn't know them from regular people."

"Sure, Amos. Whatever you say. Why don't you come in and sit down for a while? We'll talk about this later."

Chapter · 6

The owner of the Toy Emporium was a tall man with bushy gray sideburns. He introduced them to the Santa from the agency.

"Boys, this is Jim Sikes. You will be working with him today. Your job is to hand out these coloring books and prizes after Jim talks to the kids. If you have any problems, I'll be in my office."

It was difficult to tell what Jim Sikes really looked like underneath his phony white beard and glasses. One thing they could tell after they saw him in action for a while—Jim Sikes was an unpleasant man who did not like children. When he asked the little kids what they wanted for Christmas, his voice was so gruff, one little boy started to cry.

Amos gave the boy a coloring book. "Hey, cheer up, kid."

The boy cried even louder.

"Hey, kid. If you stop crying, I'll let you meet Santa's chief toy maker," Amos said.

The little boy wiped his eyes. "Really?"

"Sure. He just happens to be in the store today." Amos motioned for T.J. to come over.

"What?"

Amos leaned over to him. "I told this kid that you're Santa's chief toy maker. Show him something you made."

"I don't know. I sort of promised Dunc—"

"Dunc's not here. He's looking around for clues. Come on, T.J.—he said in case of emergency. This is an emergency. I'll explain it to him."

The little boy pulled on T.J.'s coat. "I can

tell you're the boss elf. You get to wear a coat."

T.J. beamed. "Smart kid." He led the boy to the side. "What's your name?"

"John."

"Okay, John, what I'm about to show you is top secret. We haven't actually started production on this item yet. So you can't tell anybody. Promise?"

John nodded.

T.J. pulled something out of his pocket and held it out to him.

"A ball? I've seen those before."

T.J. bounced the ball. "You've never seen one like this." Every time the ball bounced it went a little higher.

John started laughing. "Let me try! Let me try!"

T.J. reached for the ball. It got away from him. He tried to catch it, but it was out of control. T.J. chased it down the aisle. The ball kept bouncing higher and higher. "Dunc, Amos! Help!"

Dunc was in the storeroom. He noticed that the back door was open a crack. He peeked through the door and saw a delivery van outside. The side of the van said "Toys for Kids." He was about to go outside and inspect it when he heard T.J. yell.

The store had gone crazy. Everyone was screaming—except for John. He was having the time of his life. The ball was bouncing up to the ceiling and coming down harder each time, ricocheting like a bullet. Whole displays were crashing to the floor. People were taking cover under anything they could find.

Dunc grabbed a toy fishing net. He ran after the wild ball. On his third try he captured it.

The owner ran up to him, puffing and wiping sweat off his forehead. "Whose—whose ball is that?"

T.J. looked sheepish. He slid his hand up. "It's mine. I'm sorry about the damage. I'll get it cleaned up right away."

"Don't worry about the damage, son. I'll take a hundred of those balls. Right away!" He put his hand on T.J.'s shoulder and led him back to his office.

Amos grinned. "That guy will be a millionaire someday."

"Yeah, if he can live through it." Dunc said. He motioned for Amos to follow him. "I think I've found something. The back door is open, and there's a van parked outside."

"It's probably a delivery van."

"That's what I thought, at first. But the driver never gets out. He just sits there. Like he's waiting for something." He pushed the back door open a bit and looked through.

Jim Sikes was talking to the driver.

Chapter·7

"Right under our noses. I can't believe it."
Dunc tossed the newspaper to Amos, who
was rocking in Dunc's front porch swing.
"They took all the money from the cash reg-
ister while we were right there in the store.
And what's worse—we helped! We created
the perfect diversion for them with that
ball. They'll probably invite us to go along
on *all* their robberies from now on."

T.J. tried to read the latest article over
Amos's shoulder. "I feel terrible about this,

39

guys. It's all my fault. What are we going to do now?"

Amos yawned. "I vote we call the cops. We know who did it. It was that Sikes and the man in the van."

Dunc shook his head. "We only *think* we know who did it. We don't have any proof."

"It had to be them," Amos said. "It wasn't us. The store manager didn't rob himself. There wasn't anyone else."

"It could have been a customer," Dunc said. "Or it could have been your imaginary Santa."

Amos gave him a hostile look. "He's not imaginary. I saw him. He was really there. And I told you before—he didn't do it."

Dunc held up his hand. "Okay, so it wasn't that Santa. We need to figure out who it was soon, though. Christmas is in less than a week. After that . . ."

"Too bad we can't be undercover elves anymore." T.J. sighed.

"Yeah, it breaks my heart." Amos snorted.

Dunc looked thoughtful. "What's really

40

too bad is that we don't know where the agency's sending their next Santa. If we knew that, we might still have a chance."

"That's easy," T.J. said. "They're sending a Santa to Halversons, in the mall—for two days in a row, starting day after tomorrow. I heard Mr. Tyson at the agency talking on the phone."

"Are you sure?"

T.J. nodded.

Dunc clapped his hands. "All right! We're back in business. We've got two days to come up with a foolproof plan to catch these guys."

"No more disguises," Amos said. "If you guys want to look stupid in front of the whole world, go ahead, but count me out. Melissa goes into Halversons all the time. I'm not taking a chance on ruining our relationship."

Both T.J. and Dunc stared at him. Dunc spoke first. "Amos, you don't have a relationship with Melissa."

"I used to think that too. But now I know the truth. Melissa is really crazy about me."

"From what I've seen, the girl doesn't realize that you are a member of the human race." T.J. grinned.

"See?" Amos slapped his knee. "That proves my point."

Dunc pulled T.J. aside. "First he thinks he's talking to the real Santa. Now he thinks Melissa Hansen is crazy about him. He's really gone off the deep end."

Amos shook his head. "You guys don't understand the principle. Jimmy Farrel told me about it. He got it from his big brother Dennis, who has all kinds of girl-friends. Dennis says that a lot of times girls like you and they don't even *know* they like you. Sometimes they can like you for years and not know it. He says the only thing that matters is that you know that they don't know that they really like you."

T.J. whispered to Dunc, "Should we call the men in the white coats?"

"Dennis Farrel gave this to me." Amos held up a wilted piece of mistletoe. "He says girls can't resist it. Now all I have to do is wait in a place where Melissa is sure to be. And then"—he snapped his fingers—"Melissa is mine forever."

Chapter · 8

Halversons was the largest department store in the Pioneer Mall. It sold mostly expensive clothes, some jewelry, perfume, and shoes.

Dunc had called the store earlier and found out that a Santa from the agency would be on duty both days. They decided, for lack of any better disguise and because Amos was acting so weird, to pose as ordinary Christmas shoppers. But Dunc insisted that they each bring a change of clothes, so that the clerks wouldn't notice them hanging around all day.

In T.J.'s case it didn't matter whether he changed clothes or not because he insisted on wearing his trench coat, in case Dunc needed one of his inventions to help catch the crooks.

Dunc tried his best to talk him out of it. T.J. listened patiently and then quoted his great-grandmother: " 'The fly gets more to eat when he stays in the soup.' " As if that settled the whole thing.

The December morning air was crisp when they left Dunc's house. Amy had once again loaned T.J. her bike. Amos figured she must be sick.

They made good time getting to the mall. They had their bikes parked and locked by nine o'clock. The plan was for Dunc and T.J. to take the first shift watching the store. Amos's job was to go around back every so often and see if the van was waiting. If nothing happened, they would trade off in an hour.

Amos checked on the van first thing. It

wasn't there. He wandered down the mall. Most of the stores were just opening. He sat down on a bench in front of a hot dog shop.

"Are you hungry, son?"

Amos turned around. It was him—the Santa from outside the toy store. Amos swallowed. "N-no. I was just sitting here killing time."

"Mind if I sit down?"

Amos looked around. "Ah, no. Go ahead. I can't stay, though. I have something to do."

The Santa nodded. "Check the alley."

"How did you—"

The Santa smiled. "It's my business. Your friends—they don't believe in me, do they?"

Amos shook his head.

"I understand. It's the same all over. The older they get, the less they believe. It's a common problem. Comes with the terri-tory."

Amos sat and listened to Santa talk about his problems for the next forty-five minutes. Things like the high cost of materials, the elf strike, and what a rough time of year it was in general.

Out of the corner of his eye, Amos saw Dunc coming down the mall. He looked at his watch. Oh, no! He had been sitting too long. He was supposed to have checked the alley again and been at Halversons ten minutes ago to take his shift.

He stood up. "Look, I have to go now. My friend is coming, and if he finds out I've been talking to you again—"

Santa waved his hand. "Say no more. I understand." He picked up his bag and started to leave. Then he stopped, leaned over, and whispered to Amos, "Tell your friend not to worry. It won't happen today."

Amos watched Santa disappear into the crowd.

Dunc found him like that. Standing, staring after Santa. "There you are. I've been looking everywhere for you. It's your turn to watch the store."

Amos blinked. He looked at Dunc. "We're

wasting our time, you know. We might as well go on home, because nothing's going to happen today."

"It's still early, Amos. They could pull something any minute."

Amos shook his head. "Not today."

"What makes you so sure?"

"Someone who knows told me."

Dunc got excited. "One of the crooks! You overheard one of the crooks talking!"

"No. It wasn't one of them."

"Amos. Have you been talking to that crazy Santa again?"

"I told you. He knows things—things nobody else knows."

Dunc sighed. "Okay, Amos. What did he tell you this time?"

"He told me all sorts of stuff. But the most important thing was that nothing would happen today."

"He sounds more like a fortune-teller than a Santa Claus. Come on, Amos. T.J. is holding down the fort alone. We better get back."

"I'll go. Just to make you happy. But it's a waste of time."

T.J. had gotten bored while Dunc was looking for Amos and decided to try on shoes. He explained to the salesman that he needed something with a large heel so he could insert his special inventions. But the salesman kept bringing out the wrong kind of shoe. Finally T.J. took off one of his own shoes to show him what he meant.

Only he forgot about the yellow smoke bomb that was set to go off when the heel of his shoe was opened.

The shoe department filled with yellow smoke. A fire alarm went off, and the sprinklers came on.

T.J. decided not to stick around.

Amos's luck wasn't much better. Since he knew the store was safe, at least for today, he wasn't paying much attention to anything.

He remembered the mistletoe in his pocket. His thoughts turned to Melissa. He stood in front of a full-length mirror and practiced holding it over his head. A woman from the jewelry section grabbed him and planted a big sloppy kiss on his cheek.

By the end of the day, they had practically memorized everything in the store and were on a first-name basis with most of the clerks. The store closed at nine o'clock, and the crooks still hadn't tried anything. Amos very tactfully reminded Dunc that he had told him so—all the way home.

Three tired boys made their way up the stairs to Dunc's room. Amos fell on the bed, fully dressed. "Next time maybe you guys will listen to me. We could have saved ourselves a lot of time and trouble."

Dunc pulled a sleeping bag out of the closet. "Amos, haven't you ever heard of coincidence? That Santa in the mall had a fifty percent chance of being right. Besides, how could he have known what we were doing anyway? He was just guessing—trying to mess with your mind."

"He knows," Amos mumbled.

T.J. pulled a cord on the front of his trench coat. "Everybody stand clear." A swooshing sound and a couple of thumps came from the coat. T.J. slipped his arms out. An air mattress that was attached to the back of the coat unfolded on the floor.

Dunc threw him a pillow. "Is there anything you *don't* have in that coat?"

T.J. grinned. "I try to be ready for any situation."

Amos rolled over. "You have a banana split in there somewhere?"

"No, but I do have a couple boxes of freeze-dried fruit and a granola bar."

"I'll pass."

Chapter·9

Amos was dreaming. Santa was stuffing all of Amos's presents back into his black bag. Next, he stuffed in the tree and was going for the Christmas dinner.

"Wake up, Amos." Dunc grabbed a foot and shook it. Amos had obviously had a rough night. His feet were on his pillow, and his head was buried under a wad of cover at the other end. "T.J. and I have been up for an hour."

"I'm happy for both of you. Go away. Can't you see I'm sleeping here?"

"I have good news."

Amos rolled over. "Go tell somebody who cares."

"It's important!"

Amos pulled the cover off his head. "Is the country under attack? Was the president impeached? If the answer is no to either question, then it's not important."

"Is he always this hard to wake up?" T.J. asked.

Dunc nodded. "Sometimes worse. I've had to learn to be creative. Watch this."

Dunc dropped down by Amos's ear. "It's about Melissa."

Amos sat straight up. "What?"

Dunc grinned at T.J. "Works every time. Now we just go downstairs and wait."

In a few minutes Amos came down the stairs. A sheet that was caught in the back of his pants was trailing behind him.

He passed Mrs. Culpepper on the stairs. Over the years she'd almost gotten used to Amos staying overnight. She scooped up the sheet. "Rough night, Amos?"

Amos nodded.

"Dunc and T.J. are eating breakfast, if you're interested."

"Thanks."

Amos stumbled into the kitchen and sat down, propping his head up with one hand. "Did someone mention Melissa?"

"Glad you could join us," Dunc said. "We were discussing our plan of attack for to-day."

"We're attacking Melissa?" Amos said, still half asleep.

T.J. laughed. "I didn't know you were this much fun, Amos."

"How about some breakfast to help you wake up?" Dunc said.

"What is it?"

"Oatmeal."

"Yeecchh! That stuff is for horses. Where's my . . . ?"

Dunc set a box of Fruit Slams in front of him.

"That's better. Now, what are we attacking?"

Dunc cleared his throat. "We've been talking about how to keep the crooks under surveillance today—"

"Speak English," Amos growled.

"—and we think it would be best to go back undercover."

Amos shook his head. "Melissa is not going to see my skinny legs in green tights ever again in this lifetime."

"That's the beauty of our plan—actually, T.J. thought of it. Melissa will never know it's you. Guaranteed."

"Guaranteed?"

Dunc put his hand on his heart. "Trust me."

"Don't say that. I was about to go for it until you said that."

T.J. came around the table. "I promise, Amos. She won't recognize you—that is, not until after we catch the bad guys. Then you'll probably be a hero. Maybe have to go on TV to tell about it. Talk shows, the news, that kind of stuff."

Dunc winked at T.J. behind Amos's back and whispered, "You're catching on."

Chapter · 10

The boys were in the rest room at the mall.
They were helping Amos into his disguise.

"What did I do to deserve you guys?"
Amos looked at T.J. "It's bad enough coming
from my best friend. But my own cousin?"

"You were the one that didn't want to be
recognized," T.J. said. "I was only trying to
help. We called Wally's Custom Costumes,
and this was the only thing he had that he
could guarantee no one would recognize you
in. I thought you'd be happy."

"I'm supposed to be happy wearing antlers? I've gone from Peter Pan to Bullwinkle."

Dunc spoke up. "We were lucky to get the costume. It fits in with the season and everything. No one will be suspicious of one of Santa's reindeer."

"Don't you think the store will know if they ordered a reindeer or not?" Amos asked.

"That's what's so great about this plan," Dunc said. "The store will think you came with the Santa. And the Santa will think you work for the store. It's perfect. Now, get your head on. The store's about to open."

"Wait a minute—what are you two going to be doing while I'm watching the store?"

"We'll be right there with you, Amos." Dunc shoved the reindeer head down over Amos's ears. "Only not as visible as yesterday. If you see anything—yell. We'll be there in a flash. Don't worry."

They led him through the mall toward Halversons. The little kids went wild when they spotted him. One little girl grabbed his leg and wouldn't let go. He tried to shake her off. She hung on tight.

Amos bent down and whispered something to her. She let go and ran off screaming for her mother.

"What did you say to her?" Dunc asked.

"I told her that Santa lets me eat all the bad little kids for breakfast. And her name was next on the list."

Dunc tried not to smile. "She'll probably have nightmares."

"Good."

"Okay, Amos. Here's the store." Dunc straightened an antler. "You find a good spot where you can watch the Santa. T.J. and I will keep an eye out for the van."

Amos moved in near the Santa. It was Jim Sikes from the Lundini Agency. Amos found a spot on the far side of the platform and sat down. The reindeer head was heavy, so he decided to lie down. When the kids finished with Santa, they paraded by Amos and petted him.

Amos was almost asleep when he heard a familiar voice. His eyes flew open.

Melissa.

She and one of her friends were baby-sitting the little boy who was talking to Santa. Melissa was standing near the platform waiting. Then it happened. . . .

Melissa reached out her hand.

And petted him.

Amos knew it was true love. He got up on all fours to talk to her—but one of his antlers got caught in her hair. Every time he moved, he yanked her hair.

Melissa's friend finally managed to get them untangled. Melissa turned and walked away without a backward glance. The kid they were baby-sitting gave him a good hard kick in the ribs. And Melissa's friend bent his antler for good measure.

Amos sat up and watched them go. Dunc moved up behind him and whispered, "What was that all about?"

Amos let out a sigh. "She touched me, Dunc. Did you see it? I told you we had a relationship."

"She didn't know it was you. You have a reindeer suit on—remember?"

Amos sighed again. "She left me some of her hair." He took a piece off his antler and held it up. "See?"

Dunc shook his head. "Listen, Amos. Now is not the time for you to get crazy on me. T.J.'s spotted the van. Something could break loose any minute. If that Sikes guy makes a move, you stay right with him. Got it?"

"Sure."

"Amos?"

"I'm sure."

Chapter · 11

Dunc knew something was about to happen. He hoped he had everything covered. T.J. was watching the outside door. Amos was watching Sikes. He had alerted Mall Security and the store manager. All he could do now was wait.

Amos was sitting on the edge of the platform playing with a piece of Melissa's hair. He looked up. Jim Sikes was taking a break. Sikes put a sign in his chair, telling the kids Santa would be right back.

Sikes had taken breaks before. But this one was different. This time he took his bag with him. Amos quickly wiggled out of his costume and followed.

Dunc saw Amos and Sikes leave the platform and was about to follow them when he noticed two other Santas coming in from the mall entrance. Each one was carrying a bag identical to Sikes's.

So that's how they did it, Dunc thought. No wonder no one had been able to identify them.

The new Santas made sure everyone in the store saw them. They even talked to a few people to be certain.

Sikes, on the other hand, was making a quick round of the store. He shoved anything that was loose into his black bag. Amos watched him scoop in rings, watches, clothes, and china.

When Sikes was through, he set his bag down on the floor. One of the new Santas casually walked by and traded bags with him.

T.J. and Amos raced over to Dunc. "What do we do now?"

"We have to keep all three of those Santas in the store until the police get here. Amos, you take Sikes. Do whatever you have to, but don't let him leave."

Sikes had gone back to his Santa chair just as if nothing had happened. The little kids started lining up to talk to him.

Amos took his job seriously. He cut in front of the first little kid and sat down on Sikes's knee.

"You're kinda big for this, ain't you?" Sikes asked.

"I just want to make sure you know everything I want for Christmas—Santa." Amos gave him a toothy imitation grin and started rattling off his wish list.

Dunc and T.J. ran for the back door. They stood in front of it, blocking the exit.

The two new Santas walked up. The taller one said, "Excuse us, boys. We need to get through that door."

The boys didn't move.

One of the Santas reached for T.J. The alarm in his trench coat went off. The boxing glove popped out and hit the man right between the eyes. It knocked him out cold.

"It works! It really works! Did you see that, Dunc?"

The other Santa dropped the bag, pushed the boys to the side, and ran out the door.

Dunc started after him.

"Don't bother," T.J. said. "He's not going anywhere. Like my great-grandma always says, 'Stop the wind, and the eagle won't fly.'"

Dunc looked puzzled.

T.J. grinned. "I let the air out of their tires."

Chapter · 12

"Front page. Look at this, Amos. You made the front page of the newspaper." Dunc showed him the copy he'd brought over.

"I've seen it," Amos sulked.

"It's a good likeness. Everybody in town should recognize you."

"Dunc, I'm sitting on Santa's knee. My reputation is shot. I won't be able to show my face in public for the next twenty years."

"It's not that bad, Amos. You should be proud of yourself. You helped bust up a ring of thieves. Those guys will be spending Christmas behind bars."

"Maybe they'll let me join them."

Dunc sat down on the living-room couch beside Amos. "I have some news that'll cheer you up."

"An earthquake is about to swallow my house?"

"Better. I've decided to give you your Christmas present a day early."

Amos looked around. "Where is it?"

"You'll know more about it when T.J. gets back."

"You sent T.J. to buy my present?"

"No. I sent him to work out those details I was telling you about."

The front door slammed. T.J. came running in with a package in his hand. "It's all taken care of, Dunc."

"Is that my present?" Amos grabbed the package from T.J.'s hands.

"No. I found this on the porch. There wasn't a card with it, so I don't know who it's for."

Amos ripped it open. Inside was the

robot from the department store. "Thanks, Dunc. It's just what I wanted."

"That's not my present, Amos. I got you something else."

Amos scratched his head. "Then who . . ."

A small white card was in the robot's hand.

Dunc read it out loud: " 'Congratulations on your case. Thank you for still believing. S. Claus.' "

T.J. and Dunc stared at each other.

Amos looked smug. "And you guys made fun of me! Said I was crazy! Imagining things! How do you explain this?"

Dunc started to answer, but T.J. cut him off. "It's almost time for the you-know-what. You better get him ready."

"What are you guys up to?" Amos asked.

Dunc cleared his throat. "It's about your present, Amos. I tried my best to think of the one thing you want more than anything else. I think I've found it. In approximately three minutes, Melissa Hansen is going to call here."

"Melissa . . . call . . . here?"

"Hold him down, T.J. He gets like this when he thinks a phone will ring."

T.J. held him on the couch.

Dunc continued. "T.J. went over to Melissa's house and told her that someone at this number would like to buy raffle tickets from her for the Christmas bazaar. She doesn't know it's you. Do you understand so far?"

Amos was rocking back and forth. He was breathing hard, and his face was turning red.

"Is he okay?" T.J. asked.

"Yeah. It usually doesn't start until he hears the first ring." Dunc looked at Amos. "Here's how we're going to do it. Are you listening, Amos?"

Amos nodded. His tongue was hanging out of the side of his mouth.

"When the phone rings, I'm going to hold it up to your ear. No crashes. No wrecks. When you hear her voice, all you have to do is talk to her. Got it?"

Amos nodded again.

"One minute," Dunc said. "You better get a good hold on him, T.J. When that phone rings, no telling what will happen."

They waited. Dunc counted down the seconds.

Amos was sweating.

It rang.

Dunc picked it up and held it to Amos's ear.

"Hello. This is Melissa Hansen. . . . Hello?"

Silence.

Amos fell over in a dead faint.

T.J. tried to revive him.

Dunc quietly hung up the phone and smiled. "Merry Christmas, Amos."

TAKE THE CULPEPPER CHALLENGE!*

1. Do you
   - *(a)* sharpen your pencils every day and keep them sorted from longest to shortest?
   - *(b)* write with whatever you find lying around in your drawer?
   - *(c)* consider yourself lucky if your neighbor has a pencil you can borrow?

2. Is your bedroom floor
   - *(a)* so clean you could eat a meal off it?
   - *(b)* partially visible near the corners of the room?
   - *(c)* buried under so much stuff you can't remember what color it is?

3. Is your bicycle
   - *(a)* a smoothly oiled, finely tuned machine in perfect working condition?
   - *(b)* slightly squeaky so wherever you go, people can hear you coming?
   - *(c)* so junky the neighbors' cat keeps trying to bury it in the backyard?

4. Do you
   - *(a)* make your bed to army regulations—so

*You may want to answer on a separate sheet so others can take this challenge too.

75

tightly a dime could bounce off your sheets?

(b) make your bed when your mother makes you make it?

(c) need hypnosis therapy to remember the last time you made your bed?

5. Have you been known
   (a) to organize the paper clips in your desk drawer?
   (b) to find last week's homework hidden in your desk drawer?
   (c) to leave slices of pizza in your desk drawer?

6. In your bedroom, do you
   (a) rotate the posters monthly to prevent visual boredom?
   (b) convince yourself that last year's arrangement is good enough for this year to avoid the bother of changing them?
   (c) use the one poster on the back of your door for a dart board?

7. Do you
   (a) count hairs to be sure to part your hair in exactly the same place every time you comb it?
   (b) brush your hair with your hands on your way out the door?

(c)   just put on a hat in the morning rather than look in a mirror?

8. Do you
   (a)   turn in extra-credit reports along with your regular homework just to be safe?
   (b)   frantically finish your assignment before the bell rings?
   (c)   have trouble remembering if you did your homework when the teacher asks?

9. Do you
   (a)   color-coordinate everything in your closet?
   (b)   feel lucky if what you're wearing makes it to a hanger by the end of the day?
   (c)   fear for your life when you open your closet?

10. Are you
   (a)   perfectly able to answer a ringing telephone?
   (b)   nervous when the phone rings, because it might be someone you owe money to?
   (c)   hard-pressed to get to the phone without wrecking at least one room in your house?

Give yourself 10 points for every (c) response, 5 points for every (b) response, and subtract 5 points for every (a) response.

PERSONALITY KEY

If you scored LESS THAN ZERO points, then you are a dead ringer for Dunc—get out your detective kit, you may have investigative talents you haven't discovered yet.

If you scored BETWEEN ZERO AND 20 points, you're a Dunc-in-training.

If you scored BETWEEN 25 AND 60 points, you have some definite Amos tendencies (especially if you answered [c] on question #10!).

If you scored OVER 60 points, then you probably have most in common with Amos's dog Scruff!

Be sure to join Dunc and Amos in these other Culpepper Adventures:

The Case of the Dirty Bird

When Dunc Culpepper and his best friend, Amos, first see the parrot in a pet store, they're not impressed—it's smelly, scruffy, and missing half its feathers. They're only slightly impressed when they learn that the parrot speaks four languages, has outlived ten of its owners, and is probably 150 years old. But when the bird starts mouthing off about buried treasure, Dunc and Amos get pretty excited—let the amateur sleuthing begin!

Dunc's Doll

Dunc and his accident-prone friend Amos are up to their old sleuthing habits once again. This time they're after a band of doll thieves! When a doll that once belonged to Charles Dickens's daughter is stolen from an exhibition at the local mall, the two boys put on their detective gear and do some serious snooping. Will a vicious watchdog keep them from retrieving the valuable missing doll?

Culpepper's Cannon

Dunc and Amos are researching the Civil War cannon that stands in the town square when they find a note inside telling them about a time portal. Entering it through the dressing room of La Petite, a women's clothing store, the boys find themselves in downtown Chatham on March 8, 1862—the day before the historic clash between the *Monitor* and the *Merrimac*. But the Confederate soldiers they meet mistake them for Yankee spies. Will they make it back to the future in one piece?

Dunc Gets Tweaked

Dunc and Amos meet up with a new buddy named Lash when they enter the radical world of skateboard competition. When somebody "cops"—steals—Lash's prototype skateboard, the boys are determined to get it back. After all, Lash is about to shoot for a totally rad world's record! Along the way they learn a major lesson: *Never* kiss a monkey!

Dunc's Halloween

Dunc and Amos are planning the best route to get the most candy on Halloween. But their plans change when Amos is slightly bitten by a werewolf. He begins scratching himself and chasing UPS trucks—he's become a werepuppy!

Dunc Breaks the Record

Dunc and Amos have a small problem when they try hang-gliding—they crash in the wilderness. Luckily, Amos has read a book about a boy who survived in the wilderness for fifty-four days. Too bad Amos doesn't have a hatchet. Things go from bad to worse when a wild man holds the boys captive. Can anything save them now?

Dunc and the Flaming Ghost

Dunc's not afraid of ghosts, although Amos is sure that the old Rambridge house is haunted by the ghost of Blackbeard the Pirate. Then the best friends meet Eddie, a meek man who claims to be impersonating Blackbeard's ghost in order to live in the house in peace. But if that's true, why are flames shooting from his mouth?

Amos Gets Famous

Deciphering a code they find in a library book, Dunc and Amos stumble onto a burglary ring. The burglars' next target is the home of Melissa, the girl of Amos's dreams (who doesn't even know that he's alive). Amos longs to be a hero to Melissa, so nothing will stop him from solving this case—not even a mind-boggling collision with a jock, a chimpanzee, and a toilet.

Dunc and Amos Hit the Big Top

In order to impress Melissa, Amos decides to perform on the trapeze at the visiting circus. Look out below! But before his best friend for life, Dunc, can talk him out of his plan, the two stumble across a mystery behind the scenes at the circus. Now Amos is in double trouble. What's really going on under the big top?

Dunc's Dump

Camouflaged as piles of rotting trash, Dunc and Amos are sneaking around the town dump. Dunc wants to find out who is polluting the garbage at the dump with hazardous and toxic waste. Amos just wants to impress Melissa. Can either of them succeed?

Dunc and the Scam Artists

Best friends for life Dunc and Amos are at it
again. Some older residents of their town have
been bilked by con artists, and the two boys
want to look into these crimes. They meet el-
derly Betsy Dell, whose nasty nephew Frank
gives the boys the creeps. Then they notice
some soft dirt in Ms. Dell's shed, and a shovel.
Does Frank have something horrible in store
for Dunc and Amos?

Dunc and Amos and the Red Tattoos

Dunc and Amos head for camp and face two
weeks of fresh air—along with regulations, de-
merits, KP, and inedible food. But wherever
these two best friends go, trouble follows. They
overhear a threat against the camp director
and discover that camp funds have been stolen.
Do these crimes have anything to do with the
tattoo of the exotic red flower that some of the
camp staff have on their arms?